For Lyall

ISBN 978-0-545-79344-5

Copyright © 2012 by Gianna Marino. All rights reserved. Published by Scholastic Inc.,
557 Broadway, New York, NY 10012, by arrangement with Viking Children's Books,
a division of Penguin Young Readers Group, a member of Penguin Group (USA) LLC,
A Penguin Random House Company. SCHOLASTIC and associated logos are
trademarks and/or registered trademarks of Scholastic Inc.

12 11 10 9 8 7 6 5 4 3 2 1   14 15 16 17 18 19/0

Printed in the U.S.A.   08

First Scholastic printing, September 2014

Set in Ionic
Book design by Nancy Brennan
The illustrations for this book were rendered in gouache and pencil
on Fabriano Artistico paper.

TOO TALL HOUSES

GIANNA MARINO

SCHOLASTIC INC.

R abbit and Owl lived in two small houses on top of a hill.

Rabbit liked to grow vegetables in the sun,

and Owl enjoyed the view of the forest.

In the evening, they played under the twilight sky.

They were good neighbors and good friends,

until one day . . .

"Rabbit!" Owl complained.

"Your garden is growing too tall.

I can't see the forest!"

"But what can I do?" replied Rabbit.

"I have to grow my food."

So Owl began to build his house taller.

Rabbit watched and chittered his teeth.

"Owl! Look what you did!
Your house is blocking the sun
from reaching my garden!"

"But I have to see the forest,"
said Owl.

So Rabbit built his house taller, too,
and planted some vegetables on the roof.

But when Rabbit watered his rooftop plants . . .

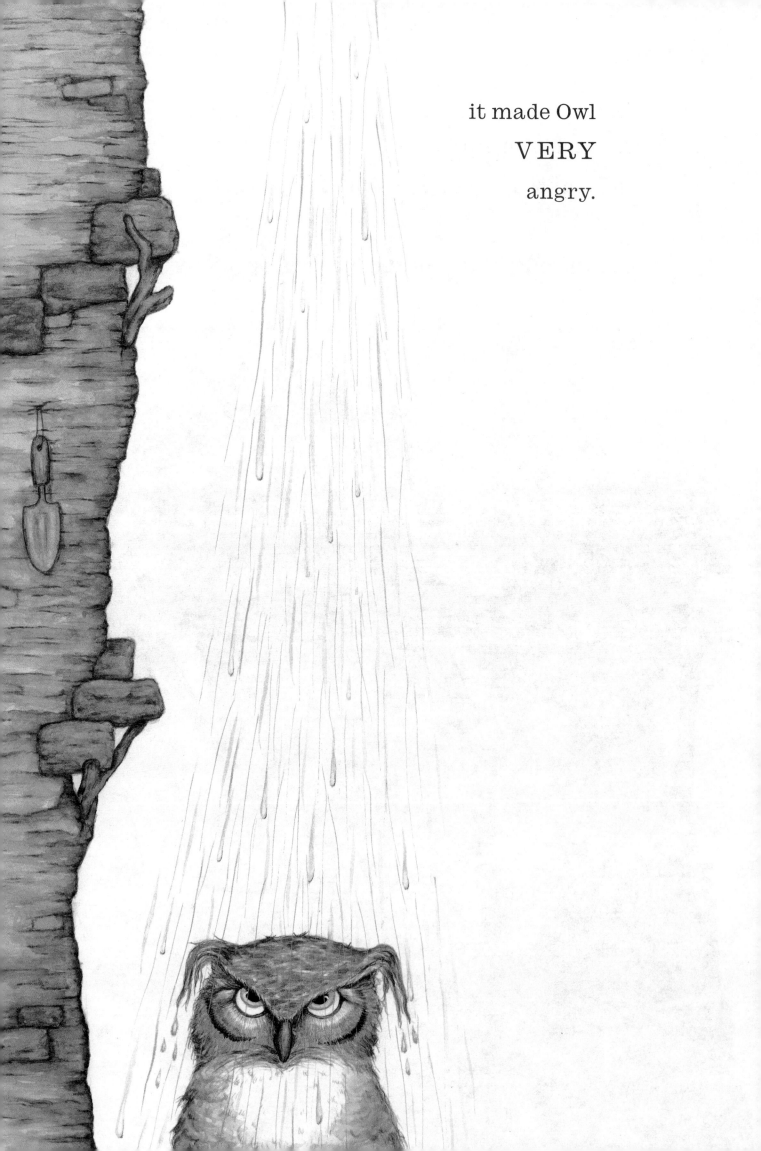

it made Owl
VERY
angry.

So Owl built his house even taller.

"I want to be the tallest!"

yelled Rabbit.

"WHAT?!" screeched Owl.
"You are so far below
me

that
I
can't
hear
you!"

So Rabbit built his house
even taller and put a fence
around his garden.

"Hoo-hoo-who do you think you are?"

screeched Owl.

And he went to find more twigs for his house.

And Rabbit went to fetch
more soil for *his* house.

And soon they had

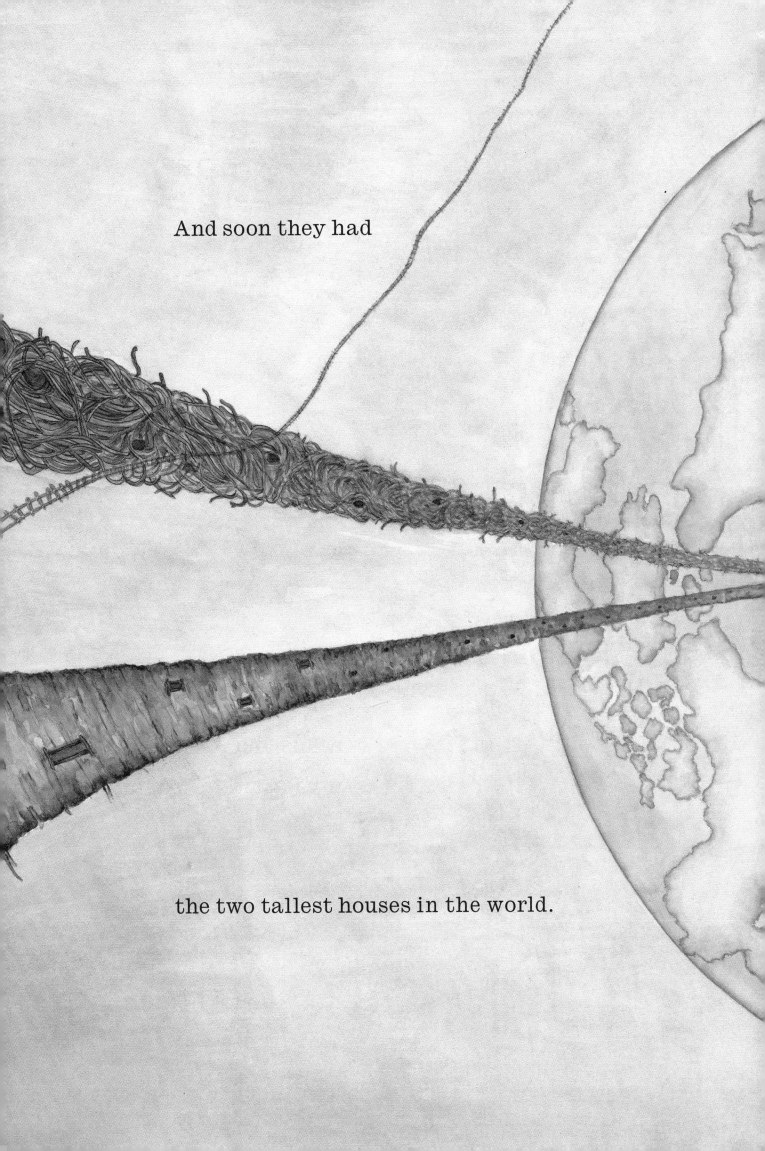

the two tallest houses in the world.

"Owl! I can't carry water
up my ladder!" cried Rabbit.

"And I can't
see the forest," said Owl.

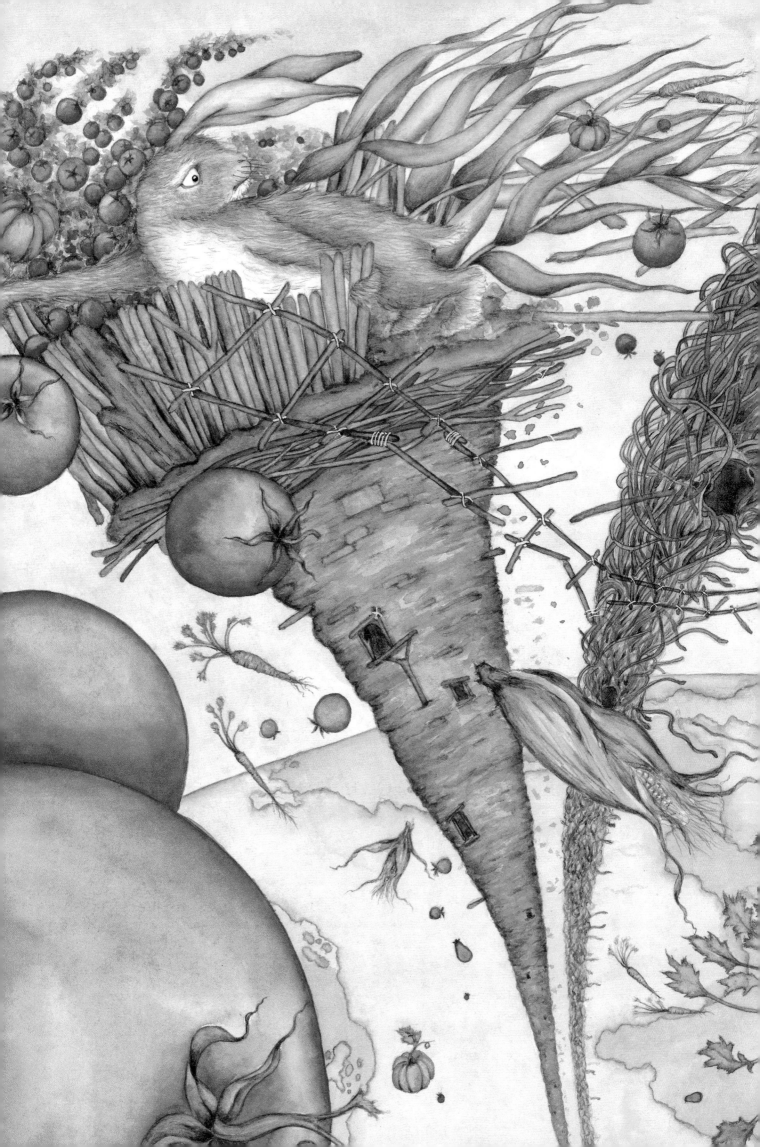

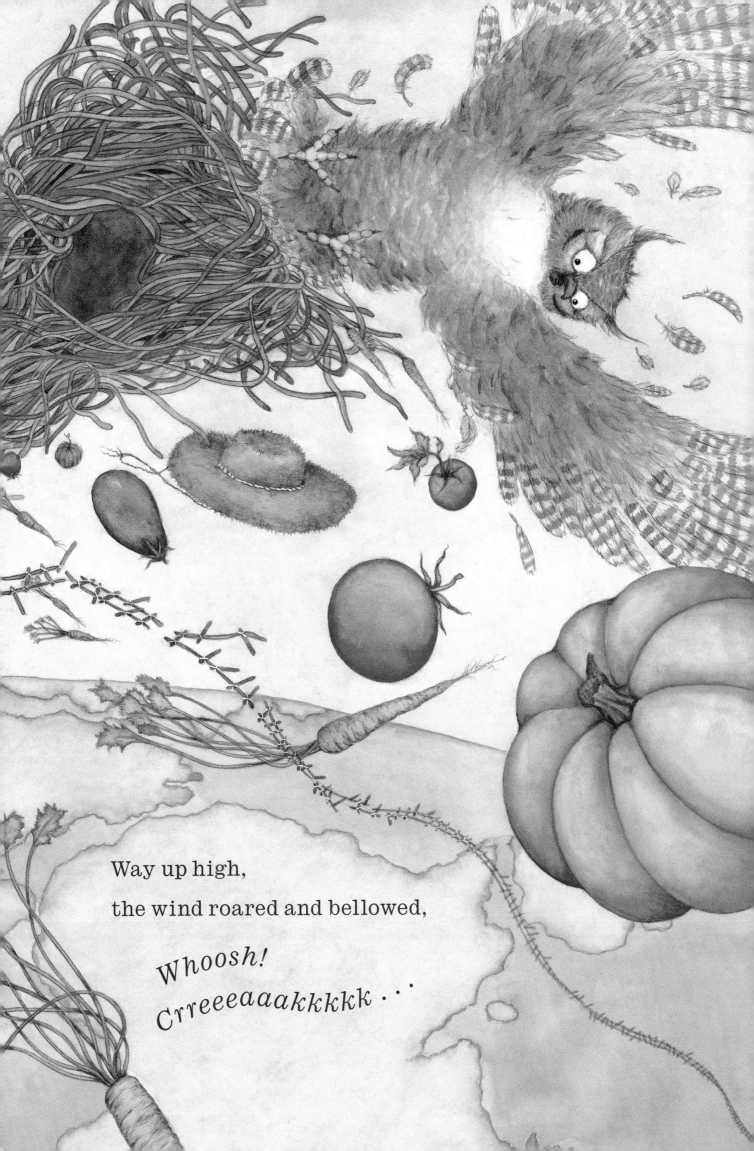

Way up high,

the wind roared and bellowed,

Whoosh!
Crreeeaaakkkkk · · ·

and blew the
too tall houses
into the air.

Crack!

Whooosh . . .

"Hold on, Rabbit!"
cried Owl.

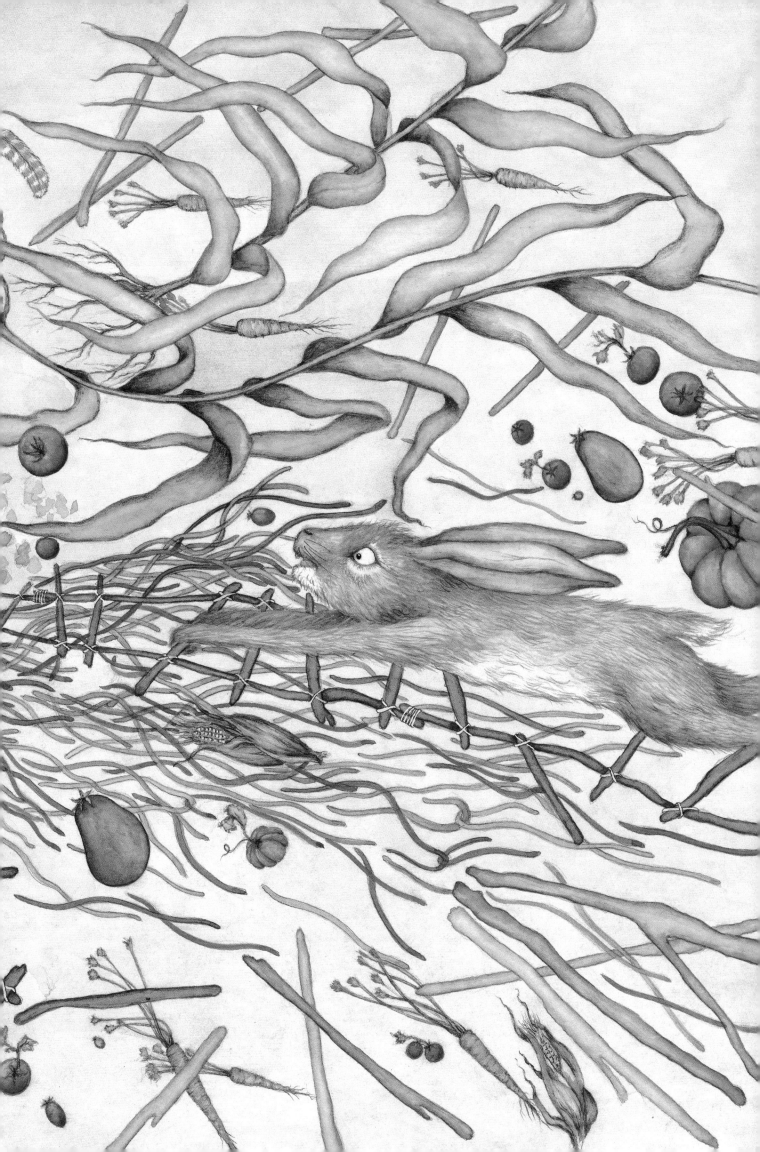

They landed with a *plunk*.

"All I have left is a pile of dirt," moaned Rabbit.

"My house is a bunch of broken twigs," sighed Owl.

Alone they had nothing . . .

but together they had all they needed . . .

to build one small house.